# .CLASSICS.
## Illustrated ®

## James Fenimore Cooper
# THE LAST OF THE MOHICANS

essay by
## June Foley, Ph. D
## New York University

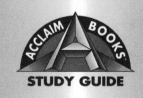

ACCLAIM BOOKS

**STUDY GUIDE**

The Last of the Mohicans
Originally published as Classics Illustrated no. 4

Art by John Severin and Stephen Addeo
Adaption by Albert L. Kanter
Cover by Alexander Maleev

*For Classics Illustrated Study Guides*
computer recoloring by Twilight Graphics
editor: Madeleine Robins
assistant editor: Valerie D'Orazio
design: Joseph Caponsacco

Classics Illustrated: The Last of the Mohicans © Twin Circle Publishing Co.,
a division of Frawley Enterprises; licensed to First Classics, Inc.
All new material and compilation © 1997 by Acclaim Books, Inc.

Dale-Chall R.L.: 6.9

ISBN 1-57848-053-8

Classics Illustrated® is a registered trademark of the Frawley Corporation.

Acclaim Books, New York, NY
Printed in the United States

# THE LAST OF THE MOHICANS

JAMES FENIMORE COOPER

IN THE SUMMER OF 1757, FRANCE AND ENGLAND WERE IN THE MIDST OF A WAR FOR POSSESSION OF NORTH AMERICA. IN THIS FIERCE STRUGGLE KNOWN AS THE FRENCH AND INDIAN WAR, MANY INDIANS WERE ALLIED WITH THE FRENCH. THEY WERE OF DIFFERENT TRIBES, BUT THE COMMON NAME FOR THEM WAS MINGO. THE OTHER EASTERN TRIBES EITHER SIDED WITH THE BRITISH OR WERE NEUTRAL. BUT ONE TRIBE HAD BEEN SO BADLY DISPOSSESSED BY THE FIRST EUROPEAN SETTLERS THAT IT HAD ALL BUT DISAPPEARED. THIS WAS THE TRIBE OF THE MOHICANS.

IT WAS THE THIRD YEAR OF THE WAR. AT THE BRITISH GARRISON, FORT EDWARD, NEAR LAKE GEORGE IN UPSTATE NEW YORK, A DETACHMENT OF SOLDIERS WAS PREPARING TO SET OUT FOR NEIGHBORING FORT WILLIAM HENRY.

WHY ARE WE MOVING, SIR?

WE HAVE REPORTS THAT GENERAL MONTCALM AND THE FRENCH ARE MARCHING ON FORT WILLIAM HENRY. COLONEL MUNRO, ITS COMMANDER, NEEDS REINFORCEMENTS.

ARE YOU MARCHING WITH US, MAJOR HEYWARD?

NO, I HAVE ANOTHER DUTY TO PERFORM.

AS THE TROOPS MARCHED AWAY, MAJOR DUNCAN HEYWARD PUSHED THROUGH A GROUP OF CURIOUS IDLERS AND ENTERED AN IMPOSING CABIN.

THAT'S THE MAJOR'S HORSE OVER THERE, SADDLED AND WAITING. BUT THE OTHER TWO ARE FITTED OUT FOR LADIES.

HE MUST BE ESCORTING THE TWO DAUGHTERS OF COLONEL MUNRO SOMEWHERE. I'VE WATCHED HIM, AND I CAN SEE THAT HE'S INTERESTED IN THE FAIR-HAIRED ONE, ALICE.

THERE THEY ARE -- AND PRETTIER GIRLS YOU'LL NEVER SEE, EH, DAVID GAMUT?

I AM A PSALM-SINGER, DEDICATED TO THE WORK OF THE LORD. THE BEAUTY OF WOMEN DOES NOT INTEREST ME. BUT IF THEY ARE GOING TO THEIR FATHER'S FORT, THEIR ROUTE DOES.

DUNCAN HEYWARD SET OUT WITH CORA AND ALICE MUNRO. AN INDIAN RUNNER DARTED PAST THEM TO LEAD THE WAY.

ARE SUCH SPECTRES FREQUENT IN THE WOODS, DUNCAN?

HE IS A RUNNER OF THE ARMY AND HAS VOLUNTEERED TO GUIDE US TO FORT WILLIAM HENRY BY A PATH BUT LITTLE KNOWN.

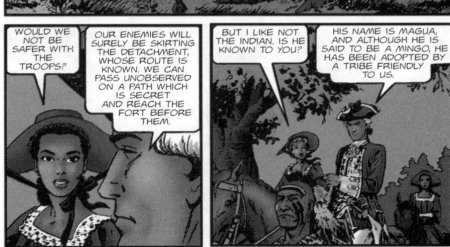

WOULD WE NOT BE SAFER WITH THE TROOPS?

OUR ENEMIES WILL SURELY BE SKIRTING THE DETACHMENT, WHOSE ROUTE IS KNOWN. WE CAN PASS UNOBSERVED ON A PATH WHICH IS SECRET AND REACH THE FORT BEFORE THEM.

BUT I LIKE NOT THE INDIAN. IS HE KNOWN TO YOU?

HIS NAME IS MAGUA, AND ALTHOUGH HE IS SAID TO BE A MINGO, HE HAS BEEN ADOPTED BY A TRIBE FRIENDLY TO US.

JUST THEN THE SOUND OF HOOFS CAUSED THE PARTY TO HALT.

WHO CAN BE FOLLOWING US?

IN A FEW MOMENTS THE FIGURE OF DAVID GAMUT CAME INTO VIEW.

SEEK YOU ANY-ONE HERE?

I HEAR YOU ARE RIDING TO FORT WILLIAM HENRY. AS I AM JOURNEYING THERE MYSELF, I CONCLUDED IT WOULD BE AGREEABLE TO HAVE GOOD COMPANY.

A MOST ARBITRARY DECISION.

THROW ASIDE THAT FROWN, DUNCAN, AND PERMIT HIM TO JOURNEY IN OUR TRAIN. HE MAY BE A FRIEND ADDED TO OUR STRENGTH IN TIME OF NEED.

DUNCAN SIGNALLED DAVID TO FALL INTO LINE, AND THE PARTY SET OUT AFTER THEIR SILENT GUIDE, UNAWARE THAT THEIR PROGRESS WAS WATCHED BY A PAIR OF WILD, FIERCE EYES.

ON THAT SAME DAY, NOT FAR AWAY, TWO MEN WERE LINGERING BY A SMALL STREAM, DEEP IN DISCUSSION.

MY PEOPLE, THE MOHICANS, WERE HAPPY, HAWKEYE, UNTIL THE PALE-FACES CAME. THEN, FOOT BY FOOT, WE WERE DRIVEN BACK FROM OUR LAND.

I AM WILLING TO ADMIT, CHINGACHGOOK, THAT MY PEOPLE HAVE MANY WAYS OF WHICH I CAN'T APPROVE.

MY TRIBE IS THE GRANDFATHER OF NATIONS. THE BLOOD OF CHIEFS IS IN MY VEINS. BUT ALL OF MY FAMILY HAS GONE TO THE LAND OF THE SPIRITS. I, TOO, MUST ONE DAY GO, AND WHEN UNCAS FOLLOWS, THERE WILL NO LONGER BE ANY OF THIS BLOOD, FOR MY SON IS THE LAST OF THE MOHICANS.

AT THAT INSTANT, A YOUTHFUL WARRIOR APPEARED.

UNCAS IS HERE! I BRING NEWS OF STRANGE MOCCASINS.

DO THE MINGOES DARE COME INTO THESE WOODS?

I HAVE BEEN ON THEIR TRAIL. THEY LIE HIDDEN LIKE COWARDS.

THE THIEVES ARE OUTLYING FOR SCALPS AND PLUNDER. DO YOU HEAR ANYTHING?

THE HORSES OF WHITE MEN ARE COMING. HAWKEYE, THEY ARE YOUR BROTHERS. SPEAK TO THEM.

IN A FEW MINUTES, THE TRAVELLERS APPEARED.

WHO COMES?

THOSE WHO SEEK FORT WILLIAM HENRY, BUT OUR GUIDE HAS LOST THE WAY.

AN INDIAN LOST IN THE WOODS! 'TIS STRANGE. IS HE A MOHAWK?

HE IS ADOPTED BY THAT TRIBE, BUT I THINK BY BIRTH HE IS A MINGO.

THEY ARE A THIEVISH RACE. A BAND OF THEM IS ABROAD TONIGHT IN SEARCH OF SCALPS, AS I THINK YOUR GUIDE KNOWS.

I WILL GO AND QUES-TION HIM.

AS DUNCAN WALKED TOWARDS HIM, MAGUA DARTED INTO THE WOODS.

DON'T FOLLOW HIM, FOR HE WOULD LEAD YOU WITHIN SWING OF THE TOMAHAWKS OF HIS COMRADES.

BUT WHAT IS TO BE DONE? DESERT ME NOT. REMAIN TO DEFEND THOSE I ESCORT.

IT WOULD NOT BE THE ACT OF MEN TO LEAVE SUCH HELPLESS CREATURES AS THESE LADIES TO THEIR FATE. THESE MOHICANS AND I WILL DO WHAT WE CAN TO KEEP THEM FROM HARM. TO TRAVEL TO THE FORT NOW THAT NIGHT IS FALLING IS DANGEROUS. BUT I KNOW A PLACE WHERE WE MAY LIE UNTIL MORNING.

*LEAVING THEIR HORSES, THE PARTY FOLLOWED HAWKEYE TO THE HUDSON RIVER, WHERE A CANOE WAS CONCEALED NEAR THE BANK. IN THE SKILLFUL HANDS OF THE SCOUT, THEY STARTED ON A PERILOUS RIDE THROUGH TURBULENT WATERS.*

WHERE ARE WE?

AT THE FOOT OF GLENN'S FALLS.

*SOON THE CANOE SHOT INTO AN EDDY AND FLOATED QUIETLY AT THE FOOT OF A FLAT ROCK.*

GO ON THE ROCK. I WILL GO BACK FOR THE MOHICANS.

WHEN HAWKEYE RETURNED WITH THE INDIANS, THEY ALL ENTERED A CAVERN IN THE ROCKS.

ARE WE SAFE HERE?

WE ARE ON AN ISLAND, WITH FALLS ON TWO SIDES OF US AND THE RIVER ABOVE AND BELOW.

NOW, YOU THAT NEED IT, SEEK FOR SLEEP. WE MUST BE AFOOT BEFORE THE SUN RISES.

OBEDIENTLY, THE SISTERS LAY DOWN UPON A COUCH OF SASSAFRAS.

CAN YOU SLEEP WITH SUCH A SENTINEL?

HE IS A FEARLESS LOOKING YOUTH. I THINK HE WILL BE A BRAVE AND CONSTANT FRIEND.

HOURS PASSED. THEN, SUDDENLY, A TUMULT OF YELLS BURST FORTH.

WHENCE COMES THIS DISCORD?

FROM MINGOES ON THE OPPOSITE BANKS. THEY HAVE SOMEHOW DISCOVERED OUR HIDING PLACE.

LEAVING THE SISTERS IN THE CAVERN WITH DAVID, THE OTHERS CREPT OUT AND *FIRED FROM THE ROCKS.*

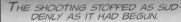

THE SHOOTING STOPPED AS SUDDENLY AS IT HAD BEGUN.

HAVE WE REPULSED THEM?

A MINGO IS NOT SO EASILY BEATEN BACK WITHOUT A SCALP.

HIST! LOOK THERE! THE RISKY DEVILS HAVE SWUM ACROSS TO OUR ISLAND.

I SEE THEM, BOYS, I SEE THEM. THEY ARE GATHERING FOR THE RUSH.

FOUR INDIANS SPRANG FROM COVER AND BOUNDED TOWARDS THEM.

HAWKEYE'S RIFLE POURED OUT ITS FATAL CONTENTS AND THE FOREMOST INDIAN FELL DEAD.

CHINGACHGOOK, KEEP US COVERED. UNCAS, TAKE THE LAST OF THE SCREECHING IMPS. WE'LL TAKE THE OTHER TWO.

A GIGANTIC MINGO LEAPED AT HAWKEYE.

FOR NEARLY A MINUTE, THEY EXERTED THE POWER OF THEIR MUSCLES.

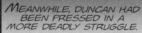

BUT THE INDIAN WEAKENED FIRST, AND HAWKEYE DROVE THE KNIFE INTO HIS HEART.

MEANWHILE, DUNCAN HAD BEEN PRESSED IN A MORE DEADLY STRUGGLE.

TOTTERING ON THE EDGE OF A PRECIPICE, DUNCAN FELT HIMSELF BEING PUSHED TO THE VERY BRINK.

JUST THEN, UNCAS APPEARED. THE MINGO RELEASED HIS HOLD AND FELL TO HIS DEATH.

TO COVER FOR YOUR LIVES! THE WORK IS BUT HALF ENDED.

THEY SOUGHT SHELTER BEHIND THE ROCKS AS A VOLLEY OF FIRE BROKE OUT FROM THE OPPOSITE SHORE.

BEFORE LONG . . .

THAT WAS THE LAST CHARGE IN MY POWDER HORN. UNCAS, LAD, GO DOWN TO THE CANOE AND BRING UP THE BIG HORN.

THE YOUNG MOHICAN COMPLIED. IN A FEW MINUTES, A LOUD CRY RANG OUT.

'TIS UNCAS! SOMETHING IS WRONG.

THE WHOLE PARTY RUSHED TO THE ROCK JUST IN TIME TO SEE THEIR CANOE BEING GUIDED INTO THE CURRENT BY AN ADVENTUROUS MINGO.

WE'RE TOO LATE! HE'S MADE OFF WITH THE POWDER!

WHAT IS TO BE DONE?

NOTHING, I FEAR, EXCEPT PREPARE TO DIE. WE ARE AT THEIR MERCY.

BUT YOU MEN HAVE THE STRENGTH TO SAVE YOURSELVES. THE RIVER COULD SWEEP YOU BEYOND THEIR REACH.

IT IS BETTER FOR A MAN TO DIE AT PEACE WITH HIMSELF THAN TO LIVE WITH AN EVIL CONSCIENCE.

BUT BY LEAVING NOW YOU MAY BE ABLE TO AID US LATER, IN THE EVENT THAT WE ARE NOT KILLED BUT ARE TAKEN CAPTIVE.

BUT SHOULD WE DIE, CARRY TO COLONEL MUNRO THE LOVE AND FINAL PRAYERS OF HIS DAUGHTERS.

YOU HAVE COURAGE, AND WHAT YOU HAVE SPOKEN IS WISE. WE WILL GO.

HAWKEYE AND CHINGACHGOOK LOWERED THEMSELVES INTO THE WATER AND WERE SWEPT DOWNSTREAM.

UNCAS REMAINED LEANING AGAINST A ROCK.

IS IT NOT TIME FOR YOU TO FOLLOW?

UNCAS WILL STAY.

GO, GENEROUS YOUNG MAN. 'TIS MY WISH, 'TIS MY PRAYER.

OBEDIENTLY, BUT GLOOMILY, UNCAS FOLLOWED.

DAVID CANNOT SWIM, BUT YOU, DUNCAN, ARE SKILLFUL IN THE WATER. SAVE YOURSELF.

YOUR WORDS ARE WASTED, CORA. I WILL NOT LEAVE.

SEEING THAT NOTHING WOULD CHANGE HIS MIND, THEY ALL RETURNED TO THE CAVERN.

FOR SOME TIME ALL WAS QUIET. THEN, A FRIGHTFUL TUMULT AROSE.

WE ARE LOST!

COURAGE. WE ARE NOT YET DISCOVERED.

THE CLAMOR INDICATED THAT THE MINGOES WERE CARRYING ON A WILD SEARCH FOR THE FUGITIVES.

THEY ARE JUST OUTSIDE!

THEN THE INDIANS RUSHED AWAY TO ANOTHER PART OF THE ISLAND.

THEY ARE GONE!

PRAISE BE TO HEAVEN FOR . . .

BUT ALICE'S WORDS DIED UPON HER TONGUE AS SHE GAZED IN HORROR AT THE ENTRANCE OF THE CAVERN.

THERE, FRAMED IN THE OPENING, WAS THE EVIL FACE OF MAGUA, THEIR TREACHEROUS GUIDE!

A SHOUT BROUGHT THE REST OF THE INDIANS.

AS RESISTANCE WAS USELESS, THE CAPTIVES WAITED WHILE THE MINGOES DELIBERATED THEIR FATE.

THE BAND OF INDIANS DIVIDED. MOST OF THEM DEPARTED, LEAVING THE PRISONERS IN THE CARE OF A FEW MINGOES LED BY MAGUA.

HE LED THEM DEEP INTO THE FOREST. WHEN THEY STOPPED TO REST...

MAGUA WOULD BE REWARDED WELL IF HE WOULD RETURN TO MUNRO HIS DAUGHTERS.

MAGUA DOES NOT WANT MONEY. GO, TELL THE DARK-HAIRED ONE I WOULD HAVE WORDS WITH HER.

CORA APPROACHED THE INDIAN.

WHAT WOULD MAGUA SAY TO THE DAUGHTER OF MUNRO?

LISTEN, WHEN MAGUA FOUGHT WITH THE BRITISH, HE DRANK FIRE-WATER AND BECAME DRUNK. MUNRO HAD HIM TIED UP LIKE A DOG.

NOW MAGUA HOLDS THE DAUGHTER OF MUNRO TO KILL, IF HE PLEASES. BUT MAGUA WISHES GREATER REVENGE. HE WISHES THE DARK-HAIRED DAUGHTER OF MUNRO TO LIVE FOR-EVER IN HIS WIGWAM.

MONSTER! ONLY A FIEND WOULD THINK OF SUCH VENGEANCE!

SO THE DAUGHTER OF MUNRO IS TOO GOOD FOR MAGUA! WE WILL SEE.

AT A WORD FROM MAGUA, ALL THE PRISONERS WERE BOUND TO TREES TO BE TORTURED.

WILL THE DAUGHTER OF MUNRO LIKE TO SEE HER SISTER DIE?

SAVAGELY, MAGUA HURLED HIS TOMAHAWK AT ALICE.

IT CUT SOME OF THE RINGLETS FROM HER HAIR. MADDENED BY THE SIGHT, DUNCAN TORE HIMSELF FREE.

HE RUSHED UPON A MINGO WHO WAS ABOUT TO REPEAT THE BLOW.

THE INDIAN SLIPPED FROM HIS HOLD, FORCED HIM BACKWARDS, AND LIFTED HIS ARM TO STRIKE.

JUST THEN, A DEADLY RIFLE SHOT RANG OUT.

THE STARTLED MINGOES LOOKED UP TO SEE HAWKEYE AND THE TWO MOHICANS.

THE CONTEST WAS HAND TO HAND.

EXTERMINATE THE VARLETS!

SOON ALL THE MINGOES WERE SLAIN EXCEPT FOR MAGUA, WHO, AGILE AS A CAT, LEAPED INTO A THICKET AND DISAPPEARED.

THE MEN HASTENED TO RELEASE THE SISTERS AND DAVID.

THE PARTY LOST NO TIME IN MAKING ITS WAY TO FORT WILLIAM HENRY, WHERE THE GIRLS WERE REUNITED WITH THEIR FATHER.

FOR THIS I THANK THEE, LORD! LET DANGER COME AS IT WILL, THY SERVANT IS NOW PREPARED.

THE WOODS ARE FULL OF FRENCH AND INDIANS, SIR. CAN THE FORT HOLD OUT MUCH LONGER?

I FEAR NOT. I AM EVEN NOW DUE AT A MEETING WITH OUR ENEMY, MONTCALM. WILL YOU COME WITH ME?

THE OPPOSING PARTIES MET IN AN OPEN SPACE IN FRONT OF THE FORT.

I TRUST YOU HAVE COME TO TREAT FOR THE SURRENDER OF THE FORT.

THIS PROTRACTED SIEGE IS BEGINNING TO IRRITATE MY FRIENDS HERE. IT IS HARD TO RESTRAIN THEIR ANGER.

MAGUA! HE HAS FOUND HIS WAY TO OUR ENEMIES!

I OFFER LIBERAL TERMS. YOU AND YOUR GARRISON MAY LEAVE IN SAFETY AND HONOR.

I MUST ACCEPT YOUR TERMS, MONSIEUR DE MONTCALM.

THE FOLLOWING MORNING, THE SILENT BRITISH ARMY MARCHED FROM THE FORT.

I MUST RIDE WITH THE TROOPS. BUT DAVID, HERE, WILL LOOK AFTER YOU.

THE COLUMNS ENTERED THE FOREST, WHERE A DARK CLOUD OF INDIANS SULLENLY WATCHED THEIR PASSAGE.

OH, CORA, IS THAT NOT MAGUA?

AT THAT MOMENT, MAGUA UTTERED AN APPALLING WHOOP. MORE THAN TWO THOUSAND RAVING INDIANS BROKE FROM THE FOREST AND THREW THEMSELVES AT THE COLUMN.

THE GIRLS STOOD, HORROR-STRUCK, WATCHING THE MASSACRE.

THIS IS NOT A FITTING PLACE TO TARRY. LET US FLY.

BUT BEFORE THEY COULD ESCAPE, MAGUA BLOCKED THE WAY.

WILL THE DARK-HAIRED ONE NOW GO TO MAGUA'S WIGWAM?

NEVER!

MAGUA CAUGHT UP THE FAINTING FORM OF ALICE AND MOVED SWIFTLY AWAY.

HOLD, WRETCH! WHAT IS IT YOU DO?

CORA FOLLOWED WILDLY, ACCOMPANIED BY THE FAITHFUL DAVID.

MAGUA LED THE WAY TO A THICKET WHERE TWO HORSES WAITED. MOTIONING CORA TO MOUNT, HE PERMITTED HER TO HOLD HER SISTER. THEN, SEIZING THE BRIDLE, HE PLUNGED DEEP INTO THE FOREST, STILL FOLLOWED BY THE PSALM-SINGER.

THREE DAYS LATER, FIVE MEN WERE SEEN SEARCHING AMONG THE DEAD THAT LITTERED THE SILENT FOREST.

MY CHILDREN! GIVE ME MY CHILDREN!

WE WILL TRY TO FIND THEM, COLONEL MUNRO.

UNCAS, WHAT DO YOU SEE?

IT IS THE VEIL OF THE DARK-HAIRED ONE.

BUT WHAT OF ALICE?

THERE ARE NO SIGNS OF HER, UNLESS THAT SHINING BAUBLE OVER THERE SHOULD PROVE ONE.

IT IS A TRINKET SHE HAD ON WHEN LAST I SAW HER!

WHAT HAVE YOU FOUND NOW, UNCAS?

I SEE THE BOOT OF THE SINGING MASTER, AND THE MOCCASIN OF MAGUA!

THEY ARE CAPTIVES OF MAGUA, THEN, AND ARE HEADED NORTH. I THINK WE CAN MOST EASILY FOLLOW BY CANOE.

HAWKEYE LED THEM TO THE NEARBY SHORE OF LAKE GEORGE, WHERE A CANOE WAS HIDDEN. TAKING THEIR PLACES, THEY BEGAN TO PADDLE NORTHWARD.

THEY CAME ASHORE NEAR THE NORTHERN END OF THE LAKE.

WE SHOULD PICK UP THEIR TRAIL ABOUT HERE.

BUT AFTER A DELIBERATE SEARCH...

THERE IS NOT A SIGN. WE MAY NOT HAVE TAKEN THE PROPER SCENT.

HERE! SEE, THE DARK-HAIRED ONE HAS GONE TOWARDS THE FROST.

'TIS THE TRAIL! THE LAD IS QUICK OF SIGHT AND KEEN OF WIT.

THE PARTY ADVANCED RAPIDLY. SOON. . .

YONDER IS OPEN SKY THROUGH THE TREE TOPS. WE ARE GETTING NIGH AN ENCAMPMENT OF MINGOES.

THEY PRESSED AHEAD. SUDDENLY. . .

AN INDIAN!

THE IMP IS NOT A MINGO. CAN YOU SEE WHERE HE HAS PUT HIS RIFLE OR HIS BOW?

HE APPEARS TO HAVE NO ARMS, NOR DOES HE SEEM VICIOUSLY INCLINED.

I WILL CREEP IN BEHIND HIM AND TAKE HIM ALIVE.

HAWKEYE CREPT UP BEHIND THE INDIAN.

BUT INSTEAD OF GRASPING HIM BY THE THROAT, HE TAPPED HIM LIGHTLY ON THE SHOULDER.

HOW NOW, DAVID GAMUT? RIGHT GLAD ARE WE TO SEE YOU SAFE.

AND I, TO SEE YOU.

A CALL BROUGHT THE OTHERS.

WHAT HAS BECOME OF MY DAUGHTERS?

THEY ARE CAPTIVES AND, THOUGH TROUBLED IN SPIRIT, ARE WELL IN BODY.

CORA IS WITH A NEIGHBORING PEOPLE WHOSE LODGES ARE BEYOND YONDER BLACK ROCK. ALICE IS DETAINED AMONG THE WOMEN OF THE MINGOES, WHOSE DWELLINGS ARE BUT TWO SHORT MILES HENCE.

YET IT IS A DANGEROUS PATH WE MOVE IN, FOR A FRIEND WHOSE FACE IS TURNED FROM YOU OFTEN BEARS A BLOODY MIND.

WHAT'S TO BE DONE?

WE WILL LET DAVID RETURN TO THE MINGO CAMP AND TELL ALICE OF OUR APPROACH.

I WILL ACCOMPANY HIM!

ARE YOU SO TIRED OF SEEING THE SUN RISE AND SET?

I WILL PASS MYSELF OFF AS A WANDERING FRENCH MEDICINE MAN, AND TRY TO EFFECT ALICE'S RESCUE, OR DIE.

VERY WELL, THE REST OF US WILL TRY TO THINK HOW BEST TO RELEASE CORA.

DUNCAN AND DAVID SET OUT AND SOON CAME TO THE MINGO CAMP.

WE WILL HEAD FOR THE LODGE YONDER WHERE THE COUNCILS ARE HELD. THE CHIEFS WILL WANT TO QUESTION YOU.

THEY ENTERED THE LODGE. SOON, A CHIEF APPROACHED.

WHO ARE YOU?

I AM A MAN WHO KNOWS THE ARTS OF HEALING. THE GREAT FRENCH FATHER SENDS ME TO YOU TO SEE IF ANY ARE SICK.

JUST THEN, A SHRILL YELL CAME FROM THE FOREST, ANNOUNCING THE RETURN OF A SUCCESSFUL WAR PARTY.

THE INDIANS GLIDED FROM THE LODGE, FOLLOWED BY DAVID AND DUNCAN.

A GAUNTLET WAS BEING PREPARED FOR A TALL AND ERECT WARRIOR WHO HAD BEEN BROUGHT IN AS A PRISONER.

INSTEAD OF RUSHING THROUGH THE HOSTILE LINES, THE PRISONER BOUNDED TOWARDS THE WOODS.

BUT HIS CAPTORS DROVE HIM BACK.

AGAIN HE DARTED FOR THE WOODS, BUT SEEING HIS WAY BLOCKED, HE TURNED AND RAN TO A SMALL, PAINTED POST WHICH STOOD BEFORE THE COUNCIL LODGE.

WHAT DOES THIS MEAN?

ANY PRISONER WHO CAN REACH THAT POST IS PRO-TECTED UNTIL THE COUNCIL HAS MET AND DECIDED HIS FATE.

DUNCAN WENT CLOSE TO THE PRISONER.

UNCAS!

THE OTHERS ARE SAFE. GO, WE MUST BE STRANGERS NOW.

DUNCAN LEFT AND WANDERED AMONG THE LODGES, LOOKING FOR ALICE. FAILING TO FIND HER, HE RETURNED TO THE COUNCIL LODGE. SOON . . .

COME WITH ME, MEDICINE MAN. I WISH YOU TO FRIGHTEN AWAY THE EVIL SPIRIT WHO LIVES IN MY DAUGHTER.

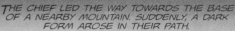
THE CHIEF LED THE WAY TOWARDS THE BASE OF A NEARBY MOUNTAIN. SUDDENLY, A DARK FORM AROSE IN THEIR PATH.

A BEAR! I HAVE HEARD THIS ANIMAL IS OFTEN DOMESTICATED BY THE INDIANS.

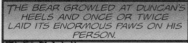
THE BEAR GROWLED AT DUNCAN'S HEELS AND ONCE OR TWICE LAID ITS ENORMOUS PAWS ON HIS PERSON.

IT FOLLOWED DUNCAN AND THE INDIAN TO A CAVE IN THE MOUNTAINSIDE.

THEY ENTERED A ROOM WHICH WAS ONE OF MANY IN THE CAVE.

NOW LET MY BROTHER SHOW HIS POWER. I GO.

DUNCAN FOUND HIMSELF ALONE WITH THE SICK WOMAN AND THE BEAR.

HOW CAN I BEST PROTECT MYSELF IF HE ATTACKS?

JUST THEN THE ANIMAL'S HEAD FELL TO ONE SIDE.

HAWKEYE! WHAT DOES THIS MEAN?

I SAW UNCAS LED INTO AMBUSH, SO I STARTED TO HIS AID. AS LUCK WOULD HAVE IT, I MET A CONJURER OF THE TRIBE IN THE ACT OF DRESSING HIMSELF IN THIS BEARSKIN.

A RAP ON THE HEAD STIFFENED HIM FOR A TIME, AND I MADE FREE WITH HIS FINERY.

BUT TELL ME, WHERE IS THE GENTLE ONE?

I DO NOT KNOW, ALTHOUGH I HAVE LOOKED IN EVERY LODGE OF THE VILLAGE.

THERE ARE OTHER CHAMBERS HERE. LET US SEPARATE AND SEARCH THEM.

SOON...

ALICE!

DUNCAN! I KNEW YOU WOULD NEVER DESERT ME.

DEAREST ALICE, MY HEART IS...

BUT DUNCAN'S TENDER WORDS WERE CUT SHORT BY A TAP ON HIS SHOULDER.

MAGUA!

UNARMED, DUNCAN DREW ALICE TO HIM AND WAITED FOR HIS DEATH.

MINGO, DO YOUR WORST. YOU AND YOUR VENGEANCE ARE ALIKE DESPISED.

AT THAT MOMENT, THE BEAR APPEARED.

GO PLAY WITH THE CHILDREN. LEAVE MEN TO THEIR WISDOM.

BUT INSTEAD OF LEAVING, THE BEAR SUDDENLY ENCLOSED MAGUA IN A MIGHTY GRASP . . .

QUICKLY, DUNCAN HELPED HAWKEYE OVERPOWER AND TIE UP THE INDIAN.

THEN, LEAVING BY THE HIDDEN ENTRANCE MAGUA HAD USED, THEY LED ALICE INTO THE WOODS.

WHEN THEY WERE SAFE...

FOLLOW THIS PATH TO THE FIRES OF THE DELAWARES AND ASK PROTECTION OF THEM. I WILL STAY AND SEE WHAT CAN BE DONE FOR UNCAS.

HAWKEYE MADE HIS WAY BACK TO A SMALL HUT ON THE OUTSKIRTS OF THE VILLAGE.

'TIS THE SINGING-MASTER!

HE SLIPPED INSIDE.

DARK MONSTER, LISTEN TO THIS INSPIRED SONG AND REPENT...

NEVER FEAR, IT IS HAWKEYE. CAN YOU PUT ME ON THE SCENT OF UNCAS?

THE YOUNG MAN IS IN BONDAGE IN A LODGE. I FEAR HIS DEATH IS DECREED.

LEAD ME TO HIM.

SIX WARRIORS GUARD HIM, BUT I DO NOT THINK THEY WILL STOP US, AS THEY ALLOW ME TO COME AND GO AT WILL.

THEY SOON ENTERED THE LODGE WHERE UNCAS LAY BOUND.

IT'S HAWKEYE, LAD. WE MUST SPEED AWAY FROM HERE AS SOON AS I THINK OF WHAT TO DO WITH THE MINGOES AT THE DOOR.

UNCAS, PUT ON THE BEARSKIN. DAVID, WILL YOU CHANGE CLOTHES WITH ME AND PLAY THE PART OF UNCAS? SINCE THE MINGOES THINK YOU ARE OUT OF YOUR HEAD, THEY PROBABLY WON'T HARM YOU.

UNCAS HAS BATTLED BRAVELY IN MY BEHALF, AND I WILL DARE THIS IN HIS SERVICE.

THE CHANGE WAS QUICKLY MADE. HAWKEYE AND UNCAS LEFT THE HUT AND WALKED TOWARDS THE WOODS.

THE DEVILS ARE LOOKING INTO THE LODGE.

LOUD CRIES ANNOUNCED THAT THE DECEPTION HAD BEEN DISCOVERED.

NOW WE MUST GO QUICKLY.

AT THE LODGE, THE ENRAGED INDIANS WERE ABOUT TO STRIKE DAVID, WHEN A BURST OF SONG FROM HIM REMINDED THEM OF HIS SUPPOSED INFIRMITY.

RUSHING OUT, THEY AROUSED THE VILLAGE.

THE INDIANS GATHERED IN THE COUNCIL LODGE TO AWAIT INSTRUCTION FROM THEIR CHIEFS.

IS MAGUA NOT HERE?

HE WENT TO THE CAVE WHERE THE SICK ONE LIES, AND DID NOT RETURN.

WARRIORS WERE SENT TO THE CAVE WHERE THEY UNTIED MAGUA AND BROUGHT HIM BACK TO THE LODGE.

WHERE ARE THE PRISONERS? LET THEM DIE!

AN EVIL SPIRIT BLINDED OUR EYES, AND THEY ESCAPED.

AN EVIL SPIRIT! NO, 'TIS THE PALE-FACE DOG THEY CALL HAWKEYE.

THEY MAY HAVE GONE TO THE DELAWARES, WHO HOLD THE DARK-HAIRED ONE FOR ME. MAGUA WILL GO AND CLAIM WHAT IS HIS.

MAGUA SET OUT WITH SOME WARRIORS, AND SOON REACHED THE DELAWARE CAMP.

MAGUA IS WELCOME. WHAT DOES HE WISH?

MY YOUNG MEN HAVE DREAMED THEY SAW THE TRAIL OF PALE-FACES NIGH THE VILLAGE OF THE DELAWARES.

THAT IS SO.

DID MY BROTHER BEAT OUT THE DOGS?

IT WOULD NOT DO. THE STRANGER IS ALWAYS WELCOME.

THE PALE-FACES ARE MY PRISONERS . . . I COME FOR MY OWN!

JUSTICE IS THE LAW OF THE DELAWARES. TAKE YOUR PRISONERS AND DEPART.

CORA, ALICE, DUNCAN, AND HAWKEYE WERE BROUGHT OUT TO THE FEET OF THE DELAWARE CHIEF.

HAVE MERCY. THERE IS ONE OF YOUR OWN PEOPLE WHO HAS NOT APPEARED. BEFORE YOU LET THE MINGO DEPART IN TRIUMPH, HEAR HIM SPEAK.

LET HIM COME.

UNCAS WAS LED OUT.

WITH WHAT TONGUE DOES THE PRISONER SPEAK?

LIKE HIS FATHERS, WITH THE TONGUE OF A DELAWARE.

I HAVE SEEN THE TRIBES OF THE DELAWARES SCATTERED LIKE BROKEN HERDS OF DEER BY THE PALE-FACES. AND NOW HERE IS A DELAWARE WHO IS LIKE A DOG OF THE WHITE MEN.

TAKE HIM AND DEAL WITH HIM!

THE DELAWARES SPRANG SAVAGELY AT UNCAS. ONE TORE HIS SHIRT FROM HIS BODY.

THE TORTOISE! THIS IS A GREAT CHIEF!

EVEN SO. MY RACE IS THE GRANDFATHER OF NATIONS, THE TRIBE FROM WHOM YOU ARE DESCENDED.

WHO ART THOU?

UNCAS, THE SON OF CHINGACHGOOK. THE BLOOD OF THE TURTLE HAS BEEN IN MANY CHIEFS, BUT ALL HAVE GONE BACK INTO THE EARTH FROM WHENCE THEY CAME EXCEPT CHINGACHGOOK AND UNCAS.

I THANK THE GREAT SPIRIT THAT YOU ARE FOUND TO FILL MY PLACE AT THE COUNCIL-FIRE.

MY SON, DOES THE MINGO SPEAK THE TRUTH? HAS HE A CONQUEROR'S RIGHT OVER YOU?

HE HAS NONE. A SNARE WAS SET FOR ME, BUT I ESCAPED.

AND THE TALL PALE-FACE?

HE LAUGHS AT THE MINGO. HE ALSO ESCAPED.

WHAT OF THE STRANGER AND THE WHITE MAIDEN THAT CAME INTO MY CAMP TOGETHER?

THEY, TOO ESCAPED.

AND THE WOMAN THAT THE MINGO LEFT WITH MY WARRIORS?

SHE IS MINE! MOHICAN, YOU KNOW THAT SHE IS MINE.

UNCAS TURNED AWAY IN SORROW.

IT IS SO.

MINGO, DEPART WITH YOUR PRISONER.

UNABLE TO INTERFERE WITH STRICT TRIBAL LAWS OF HOSPITALITY, UNCAS WATCHED ANGRILY.

MINGO, LOOK AT THE SUN. WHEN IT IS SEEN ABOVE THE TREES, THERE WILL BE MEN ON YOUR TRAIL.

UNCAS KEPT HIS EYES ON CORA UNTIL SHE WAS OUT OF SIGHT. THEN HE WENT INTO A LODGE.

AN HOUR LATER, HE REAPPEARED, PAINTED FOR BATTLE.

THE YOUNG WARRIORS OF THE DELAWARES FOLLOWED HIM IN HIS WAR DANCE.

WHEN THE SUN WAS SEEN ABOVE THE TREES, A COUNCIL WAS HELD AT THAT MOMENT. . .

IS THIS A MINGO WHO DARES APPROACH?

NO, IT IS OUR OLD FRIEND, DAVID GAMUT.

THERE IS SUCH HOWLING IN THE MINGO CAMP THAT I FLED. MAGUA HAS LEFT THE MAIDEN IN THE CAVE, AND HAS PUT HIMSELF AT THE HEAD OF HIS SAVAGES.

WHAT SAYS HAWKEYE?

GIVE ME TWENTY MEN. DUNCAN AND I WILL GO TO THE RIGHT, ALONG THE STREAM. CHINGACHGOOK AND MUNRO LIE CONCEALED THERE AND CAN JOIN US.

UNCAS, YOU DRIVE IN THE FRONT. THEN WE WILL WIN THE VILLAGE AND TAKE THE WOMAN FROM THE CAVE.

THOUGH NOT A MAN OF WAR I WILL GO WITH YOU TO STRIKE A BLOW IN BEHALF OF THE MAIDEN.

THE PARTIES SET OUT. BEFORE LONG, HAWKEYE'S BAND WAS ATTACKED BY SOME MINGOES.

JUST THEN, CHINGACHGOOK AND MUNRO APPEARED.

TAKE COMMAND, CHINGACHGOOK. I AND MY WHITE BROTHER WILL STRIKE ON FOR THE VILLAGE.

AS THEY ADVANCED, THEY SAW MAGUA WITH TWO OF HIS WARRIORS.

IS THAT UNCAS WHO RUSHES SO FEARLESSLY AFTER THE MINGO?

HE WILL OUTDISTANCE THOSE WHO WOULD HELP HIM AND FIND HIMSELF ALONE.

HAWKEYE, DUNCAN, AND DAVID FOLLOWED AS RAPIDLY AS THEY COULD.

THEY APPROACH THE CAVE!

THEY FOLLOWED THE MINGOES THROUGH THE CAVE AND OUT THE SECRET PASSAGE.

THEY HAVE CORA AND ARE DRAGGING HER WITH THEM.

UNCAS WAS GAINING ON THE MINGOES WHEN CORA SUDDENLY SHOOK HERSELF FREE.

KILL ME IF YOU WILL. I WILL GO NO FURTHER!

MAGUA RAISED HIS ARM.

JUST THEN UNCAS APPEARED ABOVE THEM AND LEAPED FRANTICALLY AT MAGUA.

AS MAGUA RECOILED, ONE OF HIS WARRIORS SLEW CORA.

UNCAS FELL PROSTRATE ON THE LEDGE AND MAGUA BURIED HIS KNIFE IN HIS BACK.

BUT UNCAS ROSE, AND WITH HIS LAST BIT OF STRENGTH, STRUCK DOWN CORA'S MURDERER.

AS UNCAS DIED, HAWKEYE, DUNCAN, AND GAMUT APPEARED ON THE LEDGE ABOVE. WITH A STONE, DAVID SLEW THE OTHER MINGO.

MAGUA ATTEMPTED TO LEAP TO SAFETY. HAWKEYE RAISED HIS RIFLE, IT POURED OUT ITS CONTENTS AND MAGUA FELL LIFELESS OVER THE PRECIPICE.

THE NEXT DAY FOUND THE DELAWARES A NATION OF MOURNERS. DELAWARE GIRLS STREWED FLOWERS ON THE GRAVE OF THE HIGH-SOULED AND COURAGEOUS CORA.

FEAR NOTHING, NOBLE MAIDEN. THE GREAT WARRIOR, UNCAS, WILL BE AT YOUR SIDE ON YOUR TRIP TO THE GREAT SPIRIT. HE WILL PROTECT YOU FROM EVERY DANGER.

THE GRIEVING MUNRO, ALICE, DUNCAN, AND DAVID RODE OFF TOWARDS THE POSTS OF THE BRITISH ARMY, LEAVING HAWKEYE AND CHINGACHGOOK AT THE GRAVE OF UNCAS.

HE WAS GOOD, HE WAS BRAVE. THE GREAT SPIRIT HAD NEED OF SUCH A WARRIOR AND HAS CALLED HIM AWAY.

HE HAS LEFT US, THE LAST WARRIOR OF THE WISE RACE OF THE MOHICANS.

THE END

# THE LAST OF THE MOHICANS

## JAMES FENIMORE COOPER

## THE AUTHOR

### "A Bundle Of Contradictions"

D. H. Lawrence called Cooper "a divided man" who lived a "double life" of "gentleman and pioneer, entrepreneur and writer, cultural elitist and cultural democrat." "The father of the novel in America," Cooper has been credited by many with creating the frontier novel, the sea novel, and the American historical romance. He was the first American novelist to support himself by his writings; and the first to gain international fame, becoming one of the most widely read authors in the world. But Cooper was also the foremost naval historian of his time, and wrote such socio-political works as *Notions of the Americans*, *The American Democrat*, and five volumes of European travel writing.

James Fenimore Cooper was born in Burlington, NJ, on Sept. 15, 1789, the 12th of William and Elizabeth Fenimore Cooper's thirteen children. Seven of the children survived childhood—James, four older brothers, and two older sisters. Cooper's father, William, rose from humble Quaker beginnings to become a man of wealth and property, acquiring large tracts of land around Lake Otsego, the source of the Susquehanna River, and founding the upstate New York settlement named for him—Cooperstown (now also site of the Baseball Hall of Fame).

In 1790 William Cooper was appointed the first judge of the Court of Common Pleas for Otsego County; and i 1795 and 1799 was elected to the U.S. House of Representatives. He was also such a formidable wrestler that he said he'd give a farm to any man who could throw him. One of James Cooper's sister said that her brothers were "very wild" and "show plainly that they have been bred in the Woods," but their mother, Elizabeth, was a genteel heiress who was said to yearn for more civilized society. James began studying at Yale College at age thirteen, but at that time seems to have resisted civilization: he was expelled in his junior year for a series of pranks, including teaching a donkey to si in a professor's chair and blowing open another boy's door with gunpowder. In 1806, James's fathe sent the seventeen-year-old to sea as a common sailor, to prepare him for a career in the navy. The year's voyage on the merchant vessel *Stirling* took him to England and Spain, and included pursuit off Portugal by a pirate ship. On returning to America James was commissioned a midshipman in the U.S. Navy on Jan. 1, 1808.

At age nineteen, Cooper inherited $50,000 as his share of his father's legac and a remainder interest in the $750,000 estate. Shortly after, he met Susan De

Lancey, the 18-year-old daughter of a prominent Westchester family—her grandfather, James De Lancey, had been chief justice and governor of New York, and leader of the New York State Loyalists to England during the Revolution. At his wife's request, after their marriage on New Year's Day, 1811, Cooper gave up his naval career.

The couple had several daughters and then two sons, one of whom died in his second year. Cooper became a gentleman-farmer of the two families' properties, moving back and forth from Westchester to Cooperstown. The collapse of the Cooper family fortune changed his life. In the depression after the War of 1812, much of the family land lost its value; it was further devalued because it was shared by four brothers who lived beyond their means and speculated unwisely. After the death of Cooper's mother in late 1818, Otsego Hall, the family home in Cooperstown, had to be sold; and by 1819 all four of Cooper's brothers had died in early middle age, leaving their families nearly destitute, and in some cases assigning James responsibility for their welfare. James attempted to recoup the family fortune by entering into several speculative ventures, including purchasing a whaler, but it was only in the least likely venture—writing—that he succeeded.

One of Cooper's "contradictions" is that the man best known as the creator of the antisocial frontiersman Natty Bumppo began his literary life as an imitator of Jane Austen! Cooper's first published fiction was a novel of manners, *Precaution* (1820), whose title even echoes Austen's last novel *Persuasion* (1818). According to his daughter Susan's account, after Cooper read the latest novel from England, he threw it aside and exclaimed, "I could write a better book than that myself." His wife "laughed at the idea, as the height of absurdity" and Cooper took this as a challenge. When *Precaution* was first published anonymously, many believed it had been written by an Englishwoman, and some critics have contended that James Cooper essentially adopted his wife's point of view in this novel. Cooper credited his wife with persuading him to write his next novel, *The Spy* (1821), the first sixty pages of which he wrote in three days. This book quickly became a popular success, and was translated into German, French, Spanish, Italian, Russian, and other languages. Cooper became famous, and referred to his wife as his "female mentor."

Another "contradiction" in Cooper is that after the great success of *The Last of the Mohicans*, this famous American author took his family on a Grand Tour of Europe. Cooper continued to write in Europe, as well as arranged with European publishers for "authorized" editions of his works that would earn him royalties, as opposed to the many pirated editions (during that time, unauthorized editions of American works were frequently printed overseas, resulting in little or no payment for the author).

However, when Cooper returned home in 1833, he found that his American readers had cooled toward him, and the United States had changed —in his view, for the worse—due to

# Cooper as Historian

Cooper's writing about the American Indians partly derived from the books he read, including Jonathan Carver's *Travels through the Interior Parts of North America* (1778), David Humphrey's *Essay on the Life of the Honorable Major-General Israel Putnam* (1778), and most importantly, two books by the Moravian missionary John Heckewelder—*An Account of the History, Manners, and Customs of the Indian Nations, Who Once Inhabited Pennsylvania and the Neighboring States...*(1818) and *A Narrative of the Mission of the United Brethren among the Delaware and Mohegan Indians...*(1820).

From Heckewelder, Cooper got the idea of the Mohicans as a diminishing, doomed tribe. He employs Heckewelder's explanation of how the Mohicans were tricked by the Iroquois into the role of "women"—counselors and peacemakers—instead of warriors. Even the name "Chingachgook" comes from Heckewelder's book. Further, Heckewelder, who lived among the Delawares, distinguishes between the noble Delawares (the Lenni Lenape or Lenape) and Mohicans (Mahicanni) and their allegedly lowly enemies the Iroquois (also called Magua, Mingwe, and Mingoes). This distinction has since been considered doubtful, but Cooper uses it as the basis of Indian conflict in *The Last of the Mohicans*.

Other historical inaccuracies or distortions that have been identified include Cooper's uncertainty about the identities of the Delaware and Mohican tribes. He confuses the Mohicans, an Algonquin tribe inhabiting the upper Hudson River almost as far north as Lake Champlain, and mainly dispersed in the 18th century, with the Mohegans, a group forming one tribe with the Pequots in Connecticut. Cooper also fails to distinguish between the Delawares and the Mohicans, even though Heckewelder does so. And Cooper's account of the Indian allegiances is wrong. During the French and Indian War, Delawares fought on the side of the French, therefore Chingachgook's loyalty belonged with them. On the other hand, the Lower Mohawk Indians aided the English, not the French, contrary to Cooper. Finally, the Huron Indians, whom Cooper vividly describes, ceased to exist nearly a century before the time depicted.

THEY ARE DELAWARES. THE MOHICANS ARE OF THE HIGH BLOOD OF THE DELAWARES, AND GREAT CHIEFS.

enormous immigration, increased materialism, and what Cooper considered the leveling of standards. In 1834 he published a pamphlet, *A Letter to His Countryman*, announcing his retirement as a novelist, criticizing American deference to foreign opinion, and defending the policies of President Andrew Jackson. The pamphlet angered the influential anti-Jackson press, which caricatured Cooper as an eccentric, embittered has-been. "This is not a country for literature," Cooper wrote to a friend, "at least not yet."

Still, Cooper could not long retire from writing. He published a satire, *The Monikons* in 1835, which found neither critical nor popular success. The next year he returned to Cooperstown and bought back Otsego Hall, recovering his family heritage. He also became involved in a controversy with the local people over their unauthorized use of Cooper land as a public picnic ground, and based a two-volume novel, *Homeward Bound* (1838) and *Home as Found* (1838), on this situation. Among the numerous works that followed are *The History of the Navy of the U.S.* (1839), the last, "dark" parts of The Leatherstocking Tales, *The Pathfinder* (1840) and *The Deerslayer* (1841), sea novels, a revolutionary-period romance, a trilogy of novels about the Littlepage family; even a play, "Upside Down" (1850), a satire on socialism. He wrote his final work, *The Towns of Manhattan*, a history of New York City, until he could

no longer hold a pen—then dictated the rest to his daughter Susan. He died on September 14, 1851, hours from age sixty-one.

## BACKGROUND
### The Leatherstocking Tales

The Leatherstocking Tales consist of *The Pioneers* (1823), *The Last of the Mohicans* (1826), *The Prairie* (1827), *The Pathfinder* (1840), and *The Deerslayer* (1841). The series title comes from one of the names of the frontiersman whom Mark Twain refers to as "Deerslayer-Hawkeye-Long Rifle-Leatherstocking-Pathfinder Bumppo."

The settings of the tales are at least as significant as their recurring characters. The stories involve the American "frontier," the farthest site of European colonization—the place where "civilization" met "savagery." Cooper wasn't the first American to write about the American frontier. In the 17th and 18th centuries, encounters between settlers and Indians and the "captivity narratives" of settlers held by Indians formed an increasingly popular literature. Cooper's fiction was also influenced by that of Charles Brockden Brown, sometimes considered the first professional American novelist. Cooper scoffed at the sensationalism of Brown's works, especially a famous cave scene in his novel *Wieland* (1799) that conveniently brought together, in Cooper's words, "an American, a savage, a wild cat and a tomahawk, in a conjunction that never did, or ever will occur." Yet Cooper followed Brown's lead in attributing to the frontier the aura of the Gothic—the mysterious and frightening, which can be linked to the "dark side" of human life and human personality.

Some scholars trace The Leatherstocking Tales back to an English work, Daniel Defoe's *Robinson Crusoe* (1717)—the work often considered the first modern novel in English. The shipwrecked Robinson Crusoe lives on a deserted island, joined only by the "savage" he saves, who becomes his loyal right-hand man, Friday. Similarly, Natty Bumppo lives in the American wilderness with his faithful Native American companion, Chingachgook. It has been noted that some artists' drawings of Crusoe—in leggings and cap, with rifle and knife—could be used to illustrate Cooper's stories of Bumppo.

The Leatherstocking Tales also have been linked with the Waverley novels of Sir Walter Scott, the most popular books of the time, not only in Scotland, the author's home and the novels' setting, but in much of Europe and North America. Cooper not only followed Scott's model of setting the stories back in history, but he adapted Scott's setting of the "neutral ground," a disputed territory on which at least two warring parties meet. Cooper even became known as "The American Scott."

But Cooper's Leatherstocking Tales differ from all their models in illustrating an idea of the American frontier that—whether truth, partial truth, or myth—became extremely influential in American life. This is the idea that the continually receding frontier became a proving ground for the colonizers; that when European civilization met Native American "savagery" and won, the result was an ever-more-powerful American civilization. It was the Englishman D.H. Lawrence, in *Studies in Classic American Literature* (1923), who defined the Leatherstocking tales as "the truth myth of America" and called Natty Bumppo "the very intrinsic-most American," because he is "a saint with a gun" who exemplifies both "the desire to extirpate the Indian" and "the contradictory desire to glorify him." Natty and Chigachgook, "two childless, womanless men, of opposite races...stand side by side..."

Natty's and Chingachgook's descendants include Herman Melville's characters Ishmael and Queequeg in *Moby-Dick*; Mark Twain's characters Huck Finn and Jim on the Mississippi, the beatnik heroes of Jack Kerouac's novel *On the Road;* the Lone Ranger and Tonto, Hawkeye Pierce and Trapper John of M*A*S*H, Butch Cassidy and the Sundance Kid—even Thelma and Louise.

ON THAT SAME DAY, NOT FAR AWAY, TWO MEN WERE LINGERING BY A SMALL STREAM, DEEP IN DISCUSSION.

MY PEOPLE, THE MOHICANS, WERE HAPPY, HAWKEYE, UNTIL THE PALE-FACES CAME. THEN, FOOT BY FOOT, WE WERE DRIVEN BACK FROM OUR LAND.

I AM WILLING TO ADMIT, CHINGACHGOOK, THAT MY PEOPLE HAVE MANY WAYS OF WHICH I CAN'T APPROVE.

One odd feature of The Leatherstocking Tales is that, in a way, Cooper wrote them backwards. *The Pioneers*, published in 1823, is chronologically the last of the novels. Here Natty is an eccentric, marginal figure, essentially powerless before the forces of civilization. At the end, he departs for the West, illustrating the inevitable American "progress." But when Cooper wrote *The Last of the Mohicans*, three years later, he made Natty younger, in vigorous middle age. The *Prairie*, published in 1827, advances the hero's age and takes him to America's Far West, where he dies, thus ending the saga—or so Cooper believed at the time. However, in 1840 Cooper resurrected Natty in *The Pathfinder*, set on and around Lake Ontario, where Cooper had served as a young man in the U.S. Navy. Although Natty is the same age as in *The Last of the Mohicans*, here he is softened by falling in love, although he fails to win the heroine, and returns to the forest with Chingachgook. The next year in *The Deerslayer* Cooper took his hero back to his youthful beginnings at wilderness adventure, in the most romantic of the tales.

# CHARACTERS

**Natty Bumppo:** Natty Bumppo has been referred to by one critic as "not a character. . .at all, but a symbol," but others maintain that the frontiersman is an individual and a symbol alike. Bumppo has many of the same sorts of contradictions as his creator, and D.H. Lawrence maintained that Cooper based Natty on himself. Bumppo first appears in *The Pioneers*, according to one critic, as "a Shakespearian fool, a grouchy buckskin buffoon with a grip on the end of his nose;" however, he leaves the book as a different man, "a superb marksman, a deeply serious figure who no longer makes

wise jokes about society. . .but is rather at odds with it."

Bumppo's "contradictions" abound in *The Last of the Mohicans*, in which the frontiersman begins as a crude figure

who boasts that he is "a man without a cross"—that he has no mixture of Indian blood in his lineage. Here Bumppo is also vengeful. His cry of "Exterminate the varlets!" seems to anticipate that of Joseph Conrad's Kurtz in "Heart of Darkness"— "Exterminate all the brutes!" Natty tells of leading an English force who surprised a smaller group of enemies, slaughtered them, and tossed the bodies of the dead and dying into the "bloody pond." That this story immediately precedes Magua's massacre of the English retreating from Fort William Henry, links Natty and Magua in vengefulness. Some critics maintain, however, that the massacre leads to Natty's transformation, and by the end he is allied with Chingachgook and noble Mohican ideals—which are, unfortunately, becoming a thing of the past.

**Chingachgook:** When the reader first meets Chingachgook, the Indian is "nearly naked;" his "expanded chest," "full-formed limbs" and "grave countenance of the warrior" all testify that he has "reached the vigour of his days." His weapons are "a tomahawk and scalping-knife, of English manufacture... a short military rifle, of that sort with which the policy of the whites armed their savage allies. . ." Yet he is a mild-mannered, intelligent, reasonable man—and more, a kind, true friend to the white Natty. He asks, "Is there no difference, Hawkeye, between the stone-headed arrow of the warrior, and the leaden bullet with which you kill?" Bumppo exclaims, "There is reason in an Indian, though nature has made him with red skin!" At Natty's request, Chingachgook tells the story of life before the English came, and moves both the frontiersman and the reader with his simple eloquence: "... we were one people, and we were happy. The salt lake gave us its fish, the wood its deer, and the air its birds. We took wives who bore us children, we worshipped the Great Spirit; and we kept the Maquas beyond the sound of our songs of triumph!" Chingachgook continues: "My tribe is the grandfather of nations, but I am an unmixed man. The blood of chiefs is in my veins, where it must stay forever. The Dutch landed, and gave my people the fire-water...Then they parted with their land..." Chingachgook's oratory builds to a climax: "Where are the blossoms of those summers!—fallen, one by one...I am on the hill-top, and must go down into the valley; and when Uncas follows in my footsteps, there will no longer be any of the blood of the

THE TORTOISE! THIS IS A GREAT CHIEF!

Sagamores, for my boy is the last of the Mohicans." Throughout the novel, Chingachgook behaves intelligently, courageously, and compassionately, all in the service of white people. Yet he wins nothing and loses everything. At the end, the noble Chingachgook himself becomes the last of the Mohicans, for his heroic son has died—and without children—foreshadowing the end of the Native Americans.

**Uncas:** Chingachgook's son is portrayed as a hero, partly by associating him with ancient Greek mythology. He is likened to Apollo, representative of youth, inspiration, and spiritual generosity, as well as physical perfection and grace. Even Uncas's "musical" speaking voice is appropriate because Apollo is the god of music. Alice Munro looks at Uncas "as she would have looked upon some precious relic of the Grecian anvil, to which life had been imparted by the intervention of a miracle," and Heyward, "openly expressed his admiration of such an unblemished specimen of the noblest proportions of man."

Uncas is also associated with Greek epic heroes, especially because of Cooper's chapter epigraphs, which come from Alexander Pope's translation of *The Iliad*. In chapter 24, the Mohicans mourn the death of Uncas, as the Trojans had mourned the death of Hector. Chingachgook, like Hector's father Priam, realizes that the loss of the hero-son means the ruin of an entire people. The death of

Uncas foretells the fate of all Indians; as early as 1757, they are doomed. As the ancient leader Tamenund put it, "The pale-faces are masters of the earth, and the time of the red-men has not yet come again. . ."

**Magua:** Magua is a "bad" Indian, and one who is "mixed." When he first appears, the colors of warpaint blend in "dark confusion," and Magua's very name means "mixed." He is an outcast from his tribe, adopted by Mohawks friendly to the English, so he pretends allegiance to the British while plotting their destruction. As the novel continues, Magua becomes increasingly vicious. He speaks in tones of "deepest malignancy" and gnashes his teeth with "rage that could no longer be bridled." His treachery reaches a climax after the surrender of Fort William Henry, as the retreating English, including many women and children, move across a plain toward the forest. It's Magua who raises the war whoop that brings barbarous bloodshed.

Yet Magua gains a kind of greatness through his association with the Satan of *Paradise Lost*, John Milton's poetic version of *Genesis*. Cooper's narrator refers to Magua as "the Prince of Darkness," and to his followers

LISTEN, WHEN MAGUA FOUGHT WITH THE BRITISH, HE DRANK FIRE-WATER AND BECAME DRUNK. MUNRO HAD HIM TIED UP LIKE A DOG.

FOR SOME TIME ALL WAS QUIET, THEN A FRIGHTFUL TUMULT AROSE.

WE ARE LOST!

COURAGE. WE ARE NOT YET DISCOVERED

as "fiends," "demons," and "devils," and Magua employs eloquent oratory much as Milton's Satan in Hell. Magua even dies by plunging from a precipice, as does Satan falls from Heaven in Milton's work. Moreover, although portrayed as malignant, Magua makes a powerful case that he was corrupted at the hands of the English, who have taken his land and then his pride, leaving him only rage.

**Duncan Heyward:** The novel is largely seen through the eyes and the point of view of Major Duncan Heyward, the handsome, young, English officer entrusted with the care of Colonel Munro's daughters, Alice and Cora. Neither a vivid nor an especially interesting character, Heyward seems hardly more than a stereotype—a "manly" white military man, sharply in contrast to the weak and timid choirmaster, David Gamut. Significantly, it is the frail and frightened Alice whom Heyward loves, not her more mature and complex sister, Cora. Moreover, he seems to love Alice not despite her fragility but *because* of it: she needs him to be her protector. At the end, the strong white man and frail white woman—Heyward and Alice—survive, to marry and populate the New World, whereas their more unconventional counterparts, Uncas and Cora, perish.

# The French and Indian Wars

*The Last of the Mohicans* takes place towards the end of the French and Indian Wars, a 70-year conflict between English and rival European colonies in North America. By the late 1600's, the claiming of the fertile New World was well under way: France possessed Canada (New France), Spain occupied Florida, and England held a string of colonies along the Atlantic seaboard. But there was still a great deal of land "available" west of the Appalachians, and this—combined with the strife among these three countries in Europe—set the stage for property disputes between colonizers, and, eventually, war.

The French and Spaniards had the advantage of relatively unified troops, in comparison to the often-squabbling English colonists. But the English made up in numbers what they lacked in unity: by the mid-1700's, the British colonies had more than 25 times as many settlers as Canada. Another important variable was the original inhabitants of these disputed lands, the Indians. Some of the tribes, often involved in their own rivalries, supported one side of the conflict over another—for example, the Delawares sided with the French, and the Iroquois sided with the English. And sometimes, as with the Iroquois, the Europeans were occasionally played off against each other—the Indians knew that the successful colonization of their lands by foreigners ultimately threatened their cultures' survival.

The French and Indian Wars were very bloody and devastating to all the peoples involved—Indian, white and black. Settlers were under constant threat of enemy raids, which often resulted in loss of property or life, and occasionally, captivity. It is one such raid that we encounter in the beginning of *The Last of the Mohicans*. The Indians also experienced death and destruction: directly in battle, or by being hunted and scalped by enterprising colonists seeking the cash bounties offered for scalps by the colonial governments (it is interesting to note that it was the *Europeans* who brought scalping to the New World).

THE OPPOSING PARTIES MET IN AN OPEN SPACE IN FRONT OF THE FORT.

I TRUST YOU HAVE COME TO TREAT FOR THE SURRENDER OF THE FORT.

Peace treaties and agreements in 1697, 1713, and 1748 temporarily halted the wars—but conflict between England, France, and Spain and the inevitable disputes over the increasing amount of land being colonized in

North America quickly put an end to the concord. Towards the end of the war, France wasn't able to give their colonists the financial or military support necessary to stay on the winning side, and the English, their Navy by this time far superior to their rivals, won. However, after so many years of fighting, all the parties involved wanted a quick end to the conflict, which had depleted their funds and morale. In 1763, the Treaty of Paris was signed, and Britain received all the land east of the Mississippi River, as well as Canada and Spain.

With the threat from France and Spain gone, the future for the English colonists seemed bright. However, the war had seriously drained Britain's economy, and heavy taxes were levied on the colonists. These settlers, rebuilding their lives after more than seven decades of off-again, on-again fighting, were not happy with this new financial burden—further, their experiences in the recent war demonstrated to them that they were quite capable of defending themselves and, if need be, surviving *independent* of Britain. Thus the outcome of the French and Indian Wars paved the way for the next big battle on north American soil...the Revolutionary War.

**David Gamut:** Washington Irving's popular character Ichabod Crane probably inspired David Gamut. Yet Gamut is also linked with the Old Testament's David, known for composing music and psalms, slaying the giant Goliath with his slingshot, and later founding the nation of Israel. Cooper's David, however, is mocked from the very beginning for his ludicrous appearance, speech, and behavior. Unlike David of the Old Testament, he remains helpless before the forces of destruction.

**Alice Munro:** The younger of the two daughters of Colonel Munro, Alice possesses a "dazzling complexion, fair golden hair, and bright blue eyes;" however, physically, intellectually, and emotionally, she is the frailer sister, an example of Cooper's heroines

BUT SHOULD WE DIE, CARRY TO COLONEL MUNRO THE LOVE AND FINAL PRAYERS OF HIS DAUGHTERS.

who have been called "uninteresting nonpersons." D.H. Lawrence referred to Alice as "the White Lily... the clinging, submissive little blonde, who is so 'pure.'" Alice's passivity endangers her and her companions, yet simultaneously renders her valuable. She seems lovable because she needs protecting. In fact, it is just such protection of frail, helpless women and their children that was used as one of the rationalizations for aggressive action by white men against Native Americans.

**Cora Munro:** Cora Munro is the daughter of Colonel Munro and a woman from the West Indies. Cora's description in the novel hints at her possible racial mix: "The tresses of this lady were shining & black, like the plumage of the raven. Her complexion was not brown, but it rather appeared charged with the

# Mark Twain on "Cooper's Literary Offenses"

One 19th-century American writer famously mocked Cooper. Mark Twain, best known today as the author of *Adventures of Huckleberry Finn*, published an essay, "Fenimore Cooper's Literary Offenses" in 1895. Criticizing mainly *The Deerslayer*, Twain contended that "There are nineteen rules governing literary art in the domain of romantic fiction—some say twenty-two," and "Cooper violated eighteen of them." Twain complained that the Leatherstocking series "ought to have been called the Broken Twig Series," because in practically every chapter, somebody is likely to "step on a dry twig and alarm all the reds and whites for two hundred yards around." Twain also referred to Cooper's hero as "Deerslayer-Hawkeye-Long-Rifle-Leatherstocking-Pathfinder-Bumppo" and claimed that Chingachgook should be pronounced Chicago. He disputed the literary critics who praised Cooper's "fullness of invention," by insisting, "Bless your heart, Cooper hadn't any more invention than a horse; and I don't mean a high-class horse, either; I mean a clothes-horse." Moreover, "Cooper seldom saw anything correctly. He saw nearly all things as through a glass eye, darkly;" and his "word-sense was singularly dull"—he "wrote about the poorest English that exists in our language." Twain mocked Cooper's loquaciousness by quoting a typical Cooper sentence —"Without any aid from the science of cookery, he was immediately employed, in common with his fellows, in gorging himself with this digestible sustenance"—and then translated it as "He and the others ate raw meat." In another essay by the writer William Dean Howells, Twain is clearly the "literary friend" asked to point out a notable heroine in Cooper's works. The 'friend" replies that Cooper's "females" were of "such extremely conventional and ladylike deportment in all circumstances that you wished to kill them.'"

colour of the rich blood, that seemed ready to burst its bounds. . ." Although the *Classics Illustrated* version of *The Last of the Mohicans* does not make this explicit, it does picture her as darker than her sister. D.H. Lawrence associated Cora's color with sexuality—he calls her "the scarlet flower of womanhood," the "dark sensual woman," "fierce" and "passionate." Other critics saw far more in Cora, however. The feminist scholar Nina Baym maintained that Cooper's multi-dimensional portrayal of Cora asks how America "might use such active traits as out-spoken bravery, firmness, intelligence, self-possession, and eloquence in a woman." Cooper's answer, according to Baym, was: "in a woman, these traits are of no use at all."

The active Cora's death and passive Alice's survival seems to suggest

that American women should exist as "protected possessions of white men."

# PLOT

The critic H. Daniel Peck has proposed that *The Last of the Mohicans* can best be understood as a journey in two parts, corresponding to the two halves of the book: the first journey moves forward in time, and the second moves into the past. The first journey moves toward Fort William Henry, in search of Colonel Munro, father of Cora and Alice, and father-*figure* to the hundreds who inhabit the fort. To Peck, Munro represents the values Cooper associates with the father as "maker of civilizations:" the commander of the fort stands at the vanguard of the European conquest of the American wilderness. Cooper therefore portrays Munro ambivalently—on one hand, as an upright, honorable, courageous man, but on the other as one who fails to protect his charges. Along with the other white, European father-figure, the French General Montcalm,

Munro shares responsibility for the massacre of women, children, the wounded, and the soldiers who have surrendered—the horrible scene that stands at the novel's center.

After the massacre, Colonel Munro becomes as helpless as his frail daughter Alice, and plays no effective role in the novel. The father figure is displaced, and the second journey begins, leading to the Delaware village, which to Peck symbolizes "Mother Nature." Here Uncas is tested and found worthy; he reveals both his spiritual ideals and the totem of the blue turtle on his chest, certifying his descent from the highest line of Mohican chiefs. Uncas's brutal murder by Magua suggests the martyrdom of Christ, and Uncas's dying without children becomes a tragedy not only for the Indians, but in a larger sense for the whole world. It is after Uncas's death that Natty Bumppo achieves fellowship with Chingachgook, according to Peck. The frontiersman and the Indian are fellow mourners in a fallen world. "Chingachgook grasped the hand that, in the warmth of feeling, the scout had stretched across the fresh earth, and in that attitude of friendship these two sturdy and intrepid woodsmen bowed their heads together, while scalding tears fell to their feet, watering the grave of Uncas like drops of falling rain."

Nearly half a century after Cooper published the last volume in the Leatherstocking series, the scholar Frederick Jackson Turner's "Significance of the Frontier in American History" put the idea of the Frontier Myth in writing. Turner defined the frontier as the meeting point in the American wilderness between "savagery" (the Indians) and "civilization" (white colonists). Further, Turner felt that American civilization *came out of the forest*—through their struggle to survive in this "untamed land" they gained the know-how and the strength to move ever westward, in what one present-day scholar has termed a continual "regeneration through violence."

THE GRIEVING MUNRO, ALICE, DUNCAN, AND DAVID RODE OFF TOWARDS THE POSTS OF THE BRITISH ARMY, LEAVING HAWKEYE AND CHINGACHGOOK AT THE GRAVE OF UNCAS.

Successive generations of Americans have reinterpreted the idea of the frontier. First the Puritans conceived their "errand into the wilderness" to bring "light"—in the form of Calvinist Christianity—into the "darkness." Then the pioneers brought "law and order" to a "savage land." In the later 19th Century, the "winning of the west" meant a return to Anglo-Saxon roots and true manhood. The idea of the frontier has been traced right down to 20th-century America's quest for the recovery of lost world power through the invasion of Asia and South America.

Cooper's Leatherstocking Tales helped create this myth, it's been suggested, by portraying the frontier as a place where civilized man can recover lost power by learning how to live with violence. Moreover, civilized man has no choice on the American frontier *but* to turn to violence, because, despite such exceptions as Chingachgook and Uncas, Native Americans are "savage" by race or blood, not responsive to civilizing; they will commit violence not just on warriors but on women and children.

In *The Last of the Mohicans*, the young English officer Duncan Heyward learns how to live with violence, thus becoming a man, the husband and protector of the surviving white woman, and the progenitor of the next Americans. This is consistent with Cooper's portrayal of the "Leatherstocking" himself, as D.H. Lawrence insisted. Natty Bumppo, "patient and gentle". . ."self-effacing" and "self-forgetting". . . . nevertheless is "a killer." Even though Natty says, "Hurt nothing unless you're forced to," Lawrence contended that this American hero "lives by death, by killing the wild things of the air and earth." As Lawrence summarized it, "The essential American soul is hard, isolate, stoic, and a killer."

## Civilization Vs. Nature

The frontier myth that advocates regeneration through violence is contradicted by the "pastoral critique" of modern European and American culture, which maintains that civilization destroys nature and spirit. And Cooper's works have been interpreted as part of this critique. Natty Bumppo declares, "Nature is sadly abused" by civilized men, once they achieve their goal of "the mastery."

Cooper remained fascinated by the idea that Native Americans did not believe in the ownership of land, even though Cooper himself held the aristocrat's view that "property is the base of all civilization," that property's "existence and security" "are indispensable to social improvement," that property "is desirable as the ground-work of moral independence, as a means of improving the faculties and of doing good to others, and as the agent in all that distinguished the civilized from the savage." That Native Americans truly did not believe in the ownership of land has been questioned by some anthropologists and historians, but it also has been widely considered *the* Native American view of nature, even by Native Americans. According to this view, the

wilderness deserves reverence as an expression of the Great Spirit; the land was created by the Great Spirit to be used by all and owned by nobody; it should not be exploited for profit or speculation, but used only for personal survival needs; and the greed of those who do not respect the land may ultimately destroy it and themselves.

To some critics, it is the pastoral critique that shapes the lives of Natty Bumppo and Chingachgook—a white man and a red man who are companions, and who choose to escape together from civilization and its discontents.

## The Mixing Of Races

Because Natty and Chingachgook are members of different races but of the same sex, their relationship, however close and loving, avoids the possibility that the two races will beget a mixed race. D.H. Lawrence and Leslie Fiedler are two prominent critics who have maintained that miscegenation is "the secret theme" of *The Last of the Mohicans*. Whether Magua lusts for Cora or intends to take possession of her mainly as revenge against her father, to Cora sexual relations with Magua seem a "fate worse than death." Yet the novel strongly hints at an attraction between the "good" characters of mixed race—Cora and Uncas. It has

BUT BEFORE THEY COULD ESCAPE, MAGUA BLOCKED THE WAY.

WILL THE DARK-HAIRED ONE NOW GO TO MAGUA'S WIGWAM?

NEVER!

been pointed out that a marriage of these two, who are certainly far more interesting than Alice and Heyward, would result in children who combine three races—white, black, and red—making America a true "melting pot." However, Cora and Uncas are both killed, and in the funeral scene at the end, even as Natty Bumppo shakes the hand of Chingachgook, "Leatherstocking" himself insists that the souls of Uncas and Cora cannot meet in the same heaven.

This seems to contradict the portrayal of Uncas throughout the novel. Uncas is shown as so heroic, in fact, that one early critic wondered "in what tribe, or in what age of history, such a civilized warrior as Uncas ever flourished?" Cooper was widely considered to have idealized Native Americans in his portrayal of Uncas, and at least one novel, William Bird's *Nick of the Woods* (1835) was published to "correct" Cooper. Recent critics have offered a more complicated interpretation of Cooper's "idealization" of Uncas: "Cooper never loves his Indians so much as when he is watching them disappear."

# STUDY QUESTIONS

• Do you feel that Natty Bumppo is more a real character or a symbol? If you feel he is more a symbol, what is he a symbol of?

• Which pair of characters do you find more interesting — Duncan and Alice, or Uncas and Cora? Why do you think one pair survives the end of the novel, and one pair does not?

• Is the comparison of Magua with the devil an apt one? Does he have any justification for betraying the English?

• Pick one pair of characters from the following list and discuss how they are alike and different: Duncan, Natty, David, Magua, Chingachgook, Uncas.

• Examine the issue of colonial expansion in America from each of the following viewpoints: The Frontier Myth and the Pastoral Critique.

• Do you think that Mark Twain's critique of Cooper's work is justified? If so, to what extent?

• Do you see the contradictions in Cooper's own life mirrored in the character of Natty Bumppo? How? Are these contradictions evident in the tone of the novel as a whole?

• If Cooper's work established the frontier tale (whether it's the frontier of Colonial America, the Wild West, or the "final frontier" of space exploration) as an important genre, can you see examples of such stories in popular culture now? What themes and traits do frontier stories share? (In other words, does Last of the Mohicans have anything in common with, for example, Star Trek?)

## About the Essayist:

June Foley holds a Ph.D. in English Literature from New York University, where she is an adjunct Assistant Professor. She is also the author of four young adult novels.